W9-CTH-146

THE ONLY LIVING BOY

TO SAVE A SHATTERED WORLD

by David Gallaher and Steve Ellis

PAPERCUTZ™

New York

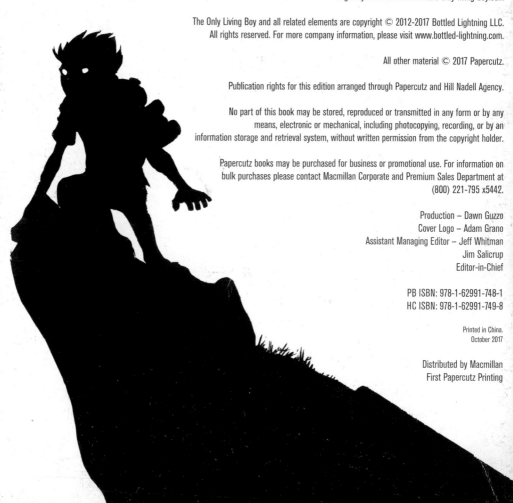

Dedicated to everyone out there
fighting the good fight.

THE ONLY LIVING BOY #5 "To Save a Shattered World"

Chapters 9 & 10
Writer/Co-Creator: David Gallaher
Artist/Co-Creator: Steve Ellis
Color Flatting: Holley McKend, Jules Rivera, Caitlin Like
Additional Flatting: David B. Cooper, Allison Strejlau
Proofreading: Janelle Asselin
Lettering: Melanie Ujimori
Assistant Editor: Emily Walton
Studio Assistant: Jen Lightfoot
Production: Salina Marie Gomez

Special Thanks to Grace Gordon and Sarah Sawyers-Lovett

Originally serialized at: www.the-only-living-boy.com

Production – Dawn Guzzo
Cover Logo – Adam Grano
Assistant Managing Editor – Jeff Whitman
Jim Salicrup
Editor-in-Chief

PB ISBN: 978-1-62991-748-1
HC ISBN: 978-1-62991-749-8

Printed in China.
October 2017

Distributed by Macmillan
First Papercutz Printing

CHAPTER
NINE

Previously in...

THE ONLY LIVING BOY

Staging a dangerous escape from the sinister lab of Doctor Once, Erik finds his freedom deep in the forest among the savage Alku. Appointed leader of this fierce tribe, Erik accidentally alerts Baalikar's nearby forces. With Kleef's guidance, Erik and his allies seek safety up North. In an effort to decipher Doctor Once's dying words, Erik travels alone through a forbidden swamp to find the answers he will need to defeat Baalikar. Stumbling upon an observatory, Erik discovers a colony of scientists that he is too late to save. Amidst the destruction, Erik vows to unite the forces of the patchwork planet together to stop Baalikar once and for all. Traveling to Mermidonia and the Groundling Empire, Erik convinces the tribes to join forces and save the Hive City of Sectuarius – but will he be too late?

...BUT IT WILL BE FUN.

WE SHOULD BE APPROACHING THE HIVE CITY SHORTLY.

DO THE REST OF YOU SEE THAT?

WHAT DO YOU THINK IT IS?

NOTHING TRAVELING THAT FAST COULD POSSIBLY BE FRIENDLY.

I CONCUR, *SISTER TESSA.* EVADE IT, BOY.

WAIT, *RAJ NOD...* I THINK--

EVADE!

NO. TRUST ME ON THIS...

IT'S THEA!

FATHER!

Baalikar metamorphed into a powerful creature, breached the hull, and demanded the secrets of the Chrysalis.

When I refused, he transformed into the *Thorned Queen.* I didn't have the strength to stop her.

HOW DO WE KNOW YOU ARE NOT BAALIKAR, TRYING TO DECEIVE US?

BAALIKAR CAN DISGUISE HER FORM...

...BUT SHE CANNOT DISGUISE HER AURA FROM US. IT IS ONE OF THE THINGS THAT KEPT US SAFE.

Not that it matters now...

The explosion has taken its toll on the Queen. Her soul is bound to every subject in the kingdom.

She has experienced every painful moment as it has happened.

...WHICH IS WHY WE NEED TO GET TO THE THRONE ROOM AND STOP BAALIKAR.

My body may be weary, but I will stand with you and fight.

QUICKLY, THIS WAY.

CHAPTER TEN

UNTIL THEA EMERGES FROM HER CHRYSALIS, OUR CITIZENS SHALL WANDER THIS WORLD AS NOMADS, SERVING OTHERS AS BEST WE CAN.

BAALIKAR WAS ABSORBED BY THE POWER OF THE CHRYSALIS.

WHAT ABOUT BAALIKAR?

WE SHOULDN'T SEE HIM AGAIN.

IF THEY DO, WE WILL BE READY.

HERE'S HOPING THE CONSORTIUM DOESN'T GROOM A NEW LEADER.

IF THIS BATTLE HAS TAUGHT US ANYTHING...

...IT IS THAT THIS ALLIANCE IS CRITICAL TO OUR WORLD.

WE MUST WORK TO DEFEND EVERY CULTURE.

WE MUST DEFEND NOT JUST OUR OWN CULTURE...

YOU TAUGHT US THAT, OUTLANDER.

ALL OF YOU HAVE A UNIQUE GIFT TO OFFER THIS WORLD... WAIT, HAVE ANY OF YOU SEEN RAJ NOD?

WATCH OUT FOR PAPERCUTZ™

Welcome to the fifth and final (for now!) THE ONLY LIVING BOY graphic novel, by David Gallaher and Steve Ellis, from Papercutz—those fearless entrepreneurs dedicated to publishing great graphic novels for all ages. I'm Jim Salicrup, Editor-in-Chief and Resident Eternal Optimist, here to offer some miscellaneous musings...

We've all just witnessed Erik Farrell's heroic journey to the Patchwork Planet and his epic battles against Doctor Once and Baalikar—pretty powerful stuff. But each and every one of us is on a journey, and we're all facing various obstacles on a daily basis. That's even true for a small independent publishing company such as Papercutz. While we've had many successes over the years, the reality is that it's very challenging to keep going. While nowhere near as deadly as what Erik faces, the obstacles we face can be pretty scary at times—after all, there's no guarantee that we'll always be in business. We have to work hard every day making sure we deliver graphic novels that you really want to see. THE ONLY LIVING BOY is a perfect example of the kind of material we love—a powerful story, brilliantly written and beautifully drawn. Writer David Gallaher and artist Steve Ellis take their work very seriously, creating a story that respects the intelligence of its audience. Working with David and Steve has been both a real honor and pleasure for us at Papercutz.

And that's why we're happy to announce a new graphic novel series from our Papercutz imprint for older audiences, Super Genius: HIGH MOON by David Gallaher and Steve Ellis. The creators of THE ONLY LIVING BOY have created a supernatural series set in the Old West, and Super Genius will be publishing it. We're mentioning it here because the audience for THE ONLY LIVING BOY includes a fair amount of fans old enough to pick up a Super Genius title, and we wanted you to be aware that it exists. But fair warning, HIGH MOON is NOT an all-ages title, and is suggested for mature audiences only.

For those wondering exactly what Super Genius is, allow me to explain... Not long ago, Papercutz introduced an imprint designed to publish material for older audiences called Super Genius. Recent titles have included the Eisner Award-nominated science-fiction series TRISH TRASH, by writer/artist Jessica Abel; an interesting reinvention of the Peter Pan story called THE WENDY PROJECT, by writer Melissa Jane Osborne and artist Veronica Fish; a beautifully painted adaptation of the Jules Verne classic THE CHILDREN OF CAPTAIN GRANT, by writer/artist Alexis Nesme; an all-new version of the legendary horror comic, TALES FROM THE CRYPT; and collected editions of LADY JUSTICE, TEKNOPHAGE, and MR HERO, all characters created by best-selling author Neil Gaiman. Super Genius even has a graphic novel coming up that will tell the true-life story of Joe Shuster, the co-creator of Superman—talk about a true Super Genius!

Fortunately, Papercutz continues to publish graphic novels that are able to beat the odds and find appreciative audiences. A few recent examples are THE LOUD HOUSE, a graphic novel series based on the award-winning, hit Nickelodeon animated series created by Chris Savino. It's about young Lincoln Loud, the only boy in a family that has eleven children. Lincoln's adventures are far more down-to-earth than Erik Farrell's, and a whole lot funnier. Unrelated, THE SISTERS focuses on just two siblings, Wendy and her younger sister Maureen, but they somehow manage to create just as much chaos as the Louds! We think you'll enjoy this series by Cazenove and William—which includes occasional flights of fancy with Wendy and Maureen imagine themselves as The Super Sisters!

I'd like to also mention HOTEL TRANSYLVANIA, THE ZODIAC LEGACY, DRACULA MARRIES FRANKENSTEIN, MANOSAURS, TROLLS, and many other Papercutz titles, but I thought I'd end with a title that may be just the thing to enjoy after five volumes of THE ONLY LIVING BOY...GUMBY! While Erik Farrell had to dig down deep into his soul to face nightmarish monsters, GUMBY is all about the joy of being alive and appreciating the simpler pleasures of life. We've assembled an all-star line-up of comics creators—Kyle Baker, Art Baltazar, Ray Fawkes, Veronica Fish, Sholly Fisch, Rick Geary, Mike Kazaleh, Jeff Whitman, Jolyon Yates, and others—to create the all-new adventures of everyone's favorite clayboy, and we hope you check it out. After suffering through all the havoc caused by Doctor Once and Baalikar, dealing with mischief created by those goofy Blockheads will be downright fun.

As hinted at above, Erik Farrell will return. And his adventure will continue. Be sure to keep your eye on papercutz.com for any news regarding THE ONLY LIVING BOY. So until we meet again, be sure to watch out for Papercutz!

Thanks, *Jim*

STAY IN TOUCH!

EMAIL: salicrup@papercutz.com
WEB: papercutz.com
INSTAGRAM: @papercutzgn
TWITTER: @papercutzgn
FACEBOOK: PAPERCUTZGRAPHICNOVELS
FAN MAIL: Papercutz, 160 Broadway, Suite 700, East Wing, New York, NY 10038

AFTERWORD

THE ONLY LIVING BOY began as an impossible idea. How does a boy and his teddy bear backpack navigate a world filled with monsters, mayhem and mad science? That impossible idea became thousands of words and illustrations – and the basis for the book you hold in your hand.

Bringing this part of the adventure to a close is something that we thought would happen in the distant future. But here we are, on the very last page – and it has never been more difficult to say goodbye.

When we look back at THE ONLY LIVING BOY – and the journey that Erik, Morgan, and Thea took together, our hearts are filled with joy. This has been an incredible adventure for us and it wouldn't be possible if it wasn't for the outstanding work of our agent, Dara Hyde, the diligence of our publicist, David Hyde, the exceptional work of our studio, the hardworking talent from the team at Papercutz, and the love from both our families and our exceptional fans – like you.

The world is an uncertain place. We are, all of us, trying to make sense of a world that makes no sense at all. That uncertainty can swallow us whole – and make us feel inadequate. The world doesn't make it easy for us to be brave. We often find ourselves too afraid to fail and too afraid to make a difference.

Erik Farrell is a scared kid who found himself too often running away from his problems. The world that he stumbled into was even more uncertain and senseless. With Bear by his side, he had to talk himself into being brave, even if it meant that he'd make mistakes. And... well, he makes a lot of mistakes. But if there is one lesson that we want you to take from this series, it is this: failure is better than never trying at all.

The world – our world – is weird, wide, and wonderful... and it's yours to explore alone or with your friends. It's okay to be scared. It's okay to be sad. It's okay to be filled with anger. Don't be afraid of your emotions, of your ambition, or even of your dreams – those are primal forces. Harness them to make the impossible possible. All you need is the certainty inside of you.

We will be back with new stories to tell. Thank you for believing in us as we told this one...

Steve Ellis